I0456635

Crisis Point

James Kemp

Castlegreen Publishing | Merstham

First published 2013 (as Mike's Thread)

Second edition 2013 (as Crisis Point)

Third edition 2014

Paperback edition 2018

ISBN 978-1-909951-03-7

Castlegreen Publishing

http://www.castlegreen.org.uk/

Merstham, Surrey, UK.

Rolling News

'Good Morning Washington, and Welcome. It's six a.m. on Saturday March 19th 2050. The Prosperity Crisis has taken some surprising turns overnight.'

The shot cuts away from the news anchor to a wide angle shot of the White House South Lawn. To the left, a couple of dozen camouflaged figures are moving towards the White House using the trees for cover. They've been highlighted by an overlay to make them easier to follow.

'Since the Russian Spaceship Prosperity crashed at ten pm last night there has been a confused response to the crisis from the White House. At midnight there came rumors that the Vice President had invoked the 25th Amendment to take over from the President. These were denied by John Barratt, the White House Chief of Staff overnight who said that President Booth was expected to speak directly with the Russian President at six this morning.'

3

The camera pans towards the Rose Garden, six US Marines in dress blues crouched in doorways and behind concrete planters fire at the advancing figures. The captioning is clear that this isn't live and that it happened about twenty minutes ago.

'The most recent development is what looks like a scratch force from the Pentagon attacking the White House. We've not been able to verify this officially, but the pictures tell their own story.'

The footage shows a number of US military guarding a convoy of civilian vehicles stopped at the vehicle entrance to the White House. The lead vehicle had the barrier is opened for it and is parked about fifty feet up from the barrier. However the second vehicle is stopped under the barrier, with a dent in the roof. Its tires are shredded and there is smoke coming from the front grille. The security guards can be clearly seen lying face down on the grass with their arms spread, guarded by a US Air Force officer and a couple of MPs.

The scene cuts forward and there is a line of military, it says a mixture of the services, lying prone on the ground outside the White House, most of whom are shooting at the White House. From within there is return fire, a couple of the Marines in blue dress can also be seen lying prone at the outer doors returning fire at the military line, as well as a Secret Service guy in a black suit shooting from a shattered window.

'We've not been able to get anyone to comment on this, neither the Pentagon nor the White House press office are answering calls. The timing of the incident means that our usual guy on the inside is still on the outside. However we've had reports of firing inside the White House as well as across the lawn.'

The image changes, with LIVE in red in the top corner. Marine One can be seen making a high gee take off from the helipad outside the Oval Office, unusually it is ejecting flares, smoke and bits of metal foil as counter-measures. It flies just above the vehicles down Pennsylvania Avenue lower than the buildings either side.

'It looks like the President has been evacuated from the White House. We can't be sure where to, we'll bring you more when we have it.'

CHAPTER ONE

The Conspiracy

Our reluctance to make the open step of acting against the democratically elected President of the United States kept us from acting until after the results of the 2048 election were known. There was always the chance that another President would reverse the decision to close down US Space Force and cut the other services in half. We hung our hopes on Patch for President.

Booth was popular in many areas where there was a clear direct link between his policies to encourage small businesses, thus creating jobs; rehabilitating minor offenders through Church sponsored charitable service in the local communities; and increased prosperity. In other areas though, people had lost out. This was especially the case for those involved in pharmaceuticals, abortion and the defense industries. The effect was uneven and it looked like he could lose this election.

So a lot of us helped out, unofficially, with the campaign for Jim Patch, a Presidential candidate that looked like he might set us back on the right path to proper representative democracy, rather than the tyranny of the unthinking majority. All the way up to the last minute it looked like he was going to win, the polls had him with a four point lead, and the swing states seemed to be going his way.

The 2048 Election was a controversial one, with an unexpected result. On election night it was much closer, Patch won some of the states handsomely, but lost others by very small margins, tens of votes in a few cases. All the way to the small hours and it came down to California to call, whichever way it went would be the winner.

Booth won California, by 98 votes. Patch got more Americans to vote for him than Booth, and there were allegations of vote rigging in California, Louisiana and Nebraska, all narrowly won by Booth. However, none of that changed the result.

We got the wrong President elected in 2048, back for his third term. It was clearly the beginning of the end for US Space Force.

A decision was made, but we needed to rotate our guys into the right posts before kicking off any action. We also needed to give the new President time to see if he intended to implement some of what we considered to be his crazier campaign proposals before we took action. We watched and waited.

While we got ready we saw that Virgin Galactic had formed a confederation with a couple of the other major players in the commercial space world. They'd called this the New Association of Space Administrators (NASA for short, stealing the name and logo of the original US space agency). They'd chosen the name in homage to the first guys that went to the moon because they were building a moon base.

We'd noticed a fair amount of activity mapping the moon and also putting navigational and communications satellites up. We'd thought

9

that had just been there to support the space tourism angle. These guys were going to make that a more permanent feature. They raised tens of billions in the markets, but with difficulty because the enthusiasm for large space technology projects was waning, partly because the US had stopped technology investment. Private investors were still much more open minded than the politicians, but they still knew that if the public wouldn't buy into it that they wouldn't get the returns on their money.

From where I sat, as the commander of the experimental Space Assault Wing, it looked very much like the guys behind the NASA moon base had been planning longer and better than we had. They put in the moon base in just under six months, although that was just their phase one. I was impressed, and so were a good number of my colleagues. We realized that we'd need to change our plans to take account of this new development.

In some ways it was going to make what we were planning less risky, as we had somewhere to fall back to if it didn't work. However, more preparation was needed, and we proceeded with making our own moon trips as part of testing the concept of space based interventions. That meant in reality we were doing reconnaissance and pre-positioning stores and other things we might need onto the lunar surface a short distance away from the existing infrastructure.

A week before Thanksgiving in 2049 my Executive Officer and I were summoned to a briefing in the Pentagon. The meeting was scheduled for the Wednesday, with the implicit assumption that we might end up working over the holiday. I wasn't happy at that prospect, for the first time in several months Mary would be back in the US and we'd managed to book a long weekend together. She told me that she had something special planned for us.

11

The instructions said we had to come prepared for a maximum security briefing of war plans. We would be going into the cocoon, our unofficial name for the top secret briefing room. No electronics of any kind were allowed, nor were paper notebooks or any other way of taking notes. If you were expected to act on something later then you would be issued a numbered and controlled version, either on a special chip or a paper version (the really seriously classified material still only came on special paper).

My battalion was based in Santa Fe, near the US Space Port. So we flew up to Washington after work on Tuesday and checked into the temporary officers accommodation at the Pentagon to ensure we were on station for the briefing.

In the morning we went to the cocoon twenty minutes ahead of the appointed hour and started to go through the security process. It took me two attempts to pass the scanner, searching through all the pockets on my flight suit before surrendering my multi-tool, flashlight and emergency rations from the survival pocket I'd forgotten to empty. I also had to surrender my name and unit patches to the guard who put them in a locker before handing me the key.

Once inside the cocoon I found General Hawkins' ADC, Colonel Hands from the Medical Center, and a couple of other staff officers that I did not recognize. A couple of minutes behind me Colonel Swinton came in with his XO and right behind him came General Hawkins, at which we all stood up.

'As you were Ladies and Gentlemen.' Hawkins waved us to sit down, taking the seat in the middle of the table himself. His ADC closed the door behind him and sealed us into the cocoon, we were now in a soundproof and electronics free bubble.

'Right, this is an off the record briefing and there won't be any notes. I'm also not doing introductions, if you don't already know each other it doesn't matter,' he said.

'We're here today for a final briefing on the

war activation plans in the event that the President is incapacitated for any reason and we suspect that a foreign power is looking to take advantage of our loss of leadership.

'You all have a role to play in ensuring the safety and security of the United States of America. Do you have any questions before I begin?' Hawkins asked.

There were no questions, and we spent the next three hours going through a number of likely scenarios and the responses that we were expected to make to them. Just before 13:00 General Hawkins dismissed us for lunch, as I rose to leave he said, 'Mike, can you stay back a moment, I've got a personal matter I want to discuss with you.'

'Sure,' I replied, sitting back down. Once the others left, closing the door behind them, the General continued,

'Son, you know why we're here, don't you?' he said. I nodded my assent.

'If we don't do something quite soon we're both out of a job. US Space Force is scheduled to be shut down before the next election. The President is sure that we can just use commercial space operators to put satellites in orbit, and that the demilitarization treaties mean that we have no reason to put military assets in orbit.

'We've already noted that he has been behaving erratically and having panic attacks and mood swings. We've carried him through those and he's now on regular medication for it. So far it hasn't been serious enough to worry anyone, but we expect that won't last long.'

'So, as far as anyone on the outside is concerned he's got a track record of mental instability, and we've been helping him deal with it?' I asked.

'That's correct,' General Hawkins said.

'So where do I come into this?' I asked.

'Well, that's why we're having this conversation. I fully expect that the President will have a serious mental breakdown during a national security incident sometime in the next few months. When he does, and I am 100% sure that he will, then we expect the Vice-President to invoke the provisions in the 25th Amendment to take over from the temporarily mentally-incapacitated President.

'When that happens we will invoke one of the war contingency plans that we have been discussing today. The most likely one is Plan Ford. So you need to ensure that your unit is prepared for that one without letting on that you expect it to be invoked in the next few months.'

'Have you briefed anyone else about this?' I asked.

'No, there are to be no general briefings, although we have updated a lot of the war contingency plans over the last couple of years. Those with specific roles are in the right places and know what they need to do. Everyone else will just be following a centrally prepared plan that was laid down years earlier, just in case.'

'I understand. I can do it without any problems, we've been practicing mobilization exercises on a monthly basis. I'll schedule some of the revisions in for the revised plan over the next few months,' I said.

'Excellent. Let's go get some lunch.'

During the lunch break I got a message from Mary, which was unusual but not unexpected. She'd got my message that I might be late for the weekend because I was in the Pentagon. It turned out she was here too.

We met up just outside the staff entrance, in the same place we used to meet years ago when we both worked in the building. Both our sessions ended early, lots of the staff were keen to be away for their long holiday weekend. We were no exception.

Mary was outside first and met me with a beaming smile and open arms.

'Hey there soldier, long time no see!' she called to me as I quickened my step to embrace her. After a few moments passed we separated, but remained holding hands.

'How have you been?' I asked.

'I've been great, but it's good to be back,' she said.

'I've missed you too. How long have we got this time?'

'That depends on you mister, I've got until Wednesday before my next briefing, and then I expect to be somewhere in the lower 48 for the rest of the year. I'll tell you more about it when we get in the car.'

'You've got a car?'

'Well how else were you expecting to get to my folks' place?'

'We're going to see your folks?'

'I thought that it was about high time that you met them, after all it's been nearly seven years.'

'Wow! That long? Who'd have guessed it?'

Mary punched my arm.

'Ow! You want to be careful about assaulting a superior officer?' I said

'You deserved it lunkhead, and besides, we're the same rank, unless they've given you the bird?'

'Not yet. Where's the car?'

'Follow me, big boy, it might be interesting,' she said, picking up her bag and towing me by the hand down the street.

'It always is,' I said.

Amazingly Mary had requisitioned an official car from the pool, it had never occurred to me to ask. At our grade there was an even chance of getting one, but when they were busy the more senior officers got priority. Captains and below had no chance. We stowed our bags and got in. Mary told the car what the destination was and activated it with her Army ID. We settled into our seats for the two hour drive that the car said we would have.

'So what were you in town for then?' Mary asked me.

'Oh, we had a session on some updated

contingency plans, nothing terribly exciting. They'll shape our exercises for the next few months. How about you?'

I always asked Mary what she was doing, but didn't often get a reply.

'Well I'm being re-assigned to finish off some work back home. I've got six weeks to become an expert in the biotech industry and then I may be going into space myself.'

'Will you be up there for long?'

'I don't know yet, I only got my first briefing today. But I expect I'll be based down near you for the next few months, on standby for my flight. It's all going to kick off very soon, and when it does, who knows how long it will last.'

'So the usual story, hurry up and wait?'

'That's it, but at least this time I'll be able to do it in the same town as you rather than in some ISO container in a random bit of the under-developed world.'

'Well that's sounds good to me.'

'Me too, and seeing as I'll be staying with you for the next three months, at a working space port, perhaps you could take me there yourself?'

'I'm sure I could get you on a flight if there is an official need for it.'

'I'll make sure of it. I'm still waiting for you to make me a member of the 100 mile high club!'

'How about the 100 miles per hour club?'

'Sounds like a good start!' Mary said, tinting the windows black...

We were finally ready to go. My senior team were all in on the plan and the junior officers had been picked for showing the right sort of attitudes. Importantly we had a range of contingency plans in place for all the outcomes that we had predicted.

All we needed now was a trigger, and that came in the shape of a stricken Russian spacecraft called Prosperity. It issued a mayday after an engine failure caused it to burn most of its fuel taking it out of orbit. This happened quite unexpectedly for us, but the duty officer on the closest orbital knew the script and did what he was supposed to. An interception missile was fired on what looked like an interception course with the stricken craft, but it missed deliberately.

This created the international crisis that we needed to get the President up into Air Force One where we would have him under our direct control and could sideline him. The primary idea was to have him use the 25th Amendment provisions to hand over control to the Vice President. This was only supposed to be temporary, but we knew that as soon as we had someone else calling the shots some of the disastrous decisions could be reversed.

In the Pentagon things started well, orders had already been prepared, and the conspirators knew what they needed to do. Those not directly involved had established procedures to follow and to them it would all look normal up until the point where the President was side-lined. At that stage we'd need to persuade them that we'd saved them, and hope that the Vice President would be suitably thankful for what we'd done and reverse some of the planned budget cuts.

Back in the space port I was busy getting my battalion into action. We were at high readiness, but that didn't mean that we could all deploy immediately, we needed at least six hours to collect together the whole battalion and move it. I could send a platoon up instantly and a company up within an hour. So we were mobilizing, just as we'd practiced dozens of times before (I'd been unpopular by making the guys do this about once a month for the last two years).

Crisis Point

CHAPTER TWO

March 20th

When we were all fully mobilized I called in to the Pentagon to report that we were ready to move. I asked for a sitrep, because I expected this to be my last call on the secure landline before we took off. Like all plans, ours hadn't survived contact with the enemy. President Booth had proved beyond doubt to the Russians that he was mentally erratic. On a call to them he'd denied everything and told them that he'd specifically ordered us to demilitarize space, which was news to all of us. The Chief of Staff had then had to call the Russian general staff to put them straight about the President.

My battalion was given the go-ahead to launch, and we started the process to get us all into orbit. The spacecraft were all lined up and the guys got into them as quickly as I had expected, given that we'd been doing this regularly for two years.

We were off on our mission.

Back on the ground President Booth was having kittens, and refused to listen to advice from anyone. I guess his mental breakdown was more severe than we'd expected. His advisers tried to get him to go on Air Force One to be in a mobile command post, but he steadfastly refused to leave the White House. Even the Secret Service agents couldn't get him to go, and they were most definitely not involved in our plans. A White House surgeon independently suggested that the President had suffered a mental breakdown and needed rest to recover from mental exhaustion.

In the end General McDonald took matters into his own hands and rounded up all the reliable people he could spare from the Pentagon. After visiting the armory he went round to the White House to scare the President into running away. It took some doing, and the Marines guarding the place put up a very convincing defense. However, the Secret Service did what they do best and hustled the President away into Marine One.

I was in the first spacecraft we launched, and my target was one of the clandestine orbital facilities that we'd built when I was in the Space Logistics Command. There were four of these, and they all had double sized crew facilities and a fuel generation system. We'd also fitted them with nukes, in addition to the space to surface missiles that were standard in all of our orbitals despite the treaties.

The four extras all had additional command nodes in them that could over-ride the ground based ones. They also allowed us full access to the military satellites to do with as we pleased. With these orbital facilities secure we could isolate any US Military units that didn't conform to the plan, and even feed disinformation to units. This was the key to success, and it would make a huge difference to the success or otherwise of the conspiracy.

We approached on a normal trajectory. I was feeling nervous. Even though I knew that the guys inside wouldn't fire on us, because to them we looked like a war surge of reinforcements, which they'd have seen legitimately ordered by the Pentagon. However, I was worried that they'd know there was a conspiracy to overthrow the President and they'd shoot us down as they had remained loyal to the President rather than joining in our mutiny.

From launch to being in docking range only took four minutes, but it was a long, long, time. I spent it all waiting for the missile launch. Even on docking I was expecting a burst of machine gun fire or a frag grenade through the airlock. So it was both an anticlimax and a relief when the hatch opened and I was greeted by the smiling face of one of my soldiers who we'd recently posted to the orbital crew.

As per SOP he was one of five crew on board, two were in the command deck at all times, he was the relief crewman to cover for meal breaks and trips to the heads. The other two were asleep in their bunks, and the shift change wasn't expected for another two hours.

My team took over the command deck and occupied the spare seats, in a crisis up to eight people can use the command controls, although only two are required. The standard orbitals only have seats for five, and bunks for ten. On a surge each of them is supposed to be reinforced by ten crew, including a second commissioned officer. All we had to do now was wait.

I didn't have to wait very long for something to happen. The Warrant Officer who'd been in charge of this station before I'd arrived returned from the habitation module a few minutes after we'd got ourselves squared away. I noticed that she was holding a small sealed package.

'Sir, are you Colonel Duff?' she asked

'Yes, Warrant Officer Twoomey, why do you ask?'

'Well sir, I have a package for you, arrived two days ago on a cargo flight. It was inside a larger pouch with instructions for me to hold it as you would be my relieving officer. Got to say it surprised me, usually I get relieved by another Warrant or an L.T.'

'Someone obviously knew something was likely to kick off I guess'.

She handed me the packet. Before breaking the seal on it, I took a closer look. It bore no indications of where it was from on the outside. The usual return address section was blank. It was about the size of a sheet of letter paper folded in half, and from the feel of it there were a number of non-paper enclosures.

I opened it to find two sheets of letter paper, a couple of full-bird Colonel's eagles (which explained why the address on the front had been to 'Colonel' Duff rather than 'Lt. Colonel' Duff. Also enclosed was a smaller unpadded envelope. I read the letters, the top one was a standard letter telling me that, effective 1st March 2050, I was promoted from Lt Col to full Colonel. The second was more interesting, it was a personal letter from General Hawkins, the Joint Chief of Staff, and my old boss when I'd been his ADC as a Captain. He had written the letter appointing me in the temporary role of Acting Brigadier General in local Command of all US forces above the space line 100 kilometers up.

Before I could absorb this, or open the smaller envelope, a call came in for me from the Pentagon. It was General Hawkins.

'Mike! I hope you've got the package,' Hawkins said.

'Yes sir! Just opened it a moment ago.' I held up the contents so he could see them on camera.

'Excellent! I've got a job for you, and that's why I sent you a Star. We need a General in space to persuade some people that we're really serious about what we're doing. Also, with a star on your shoulder you get to do some stuff under UCMJ that you can't do as a Colonel. Hopefully none of it will be necessary, but I want you to be ready for it if it is.'

'I'm ready for anything sir.'

'Glad to hear it. Keep in touch, and I'm sure we'll come through this fine.'

That last was clearly for the soldiers that Hawkins knew would be watching this conversation. Hawkins was no slouch, and understood the importance of morale and looking after his soldiers at all costs. He'd spent time in combat as a junior officer before we'd left all our foreign entanglements. Not many of the Generals these days had actually seen action, he was one of the last. You could certainly tell the difference in how they operated.

The next day or so was spent in watching troop movements, ours and everyone else's, and trying to keep up with the political situation earth side. It appeared to us that the whole world had mobilized for war, on the back of the US mobilization. Politically the Vice-President, Sec Def and most of the rest of the cabinet had attempted to remove President Booth temporarily using the 25th amendment and claiming that his mental state wasn't sufficient for the duties of President. Congress had accepted this, although President Booth had then used the same provisions to say that he was fine, needing another note from the Vice-President to the contrary. Now it was in the hands of Congress who had 21 days to make up their decision. However there was also a constitutional dispute about who ought to be in charge for those 21 days. Most people thought it was the Vice-President, but some sided with President Booth.

That was where we came in. We'd foreseen this level of confusion, and also the possibility that things might not go completely smoothly. So our job top side was to watch the comms between the various unit commanders and others to see where their loyalties lay. As expected most of the Air Force and the Navy were 100% behind the Vice-President and following orders from the Pentagon as normal. The State National Guards were a bit trickier, they took their normal chain of command from the Governors, only feeding into Pentagon command when they were federalized for some operational necessity. The Army units were also mostly OK, although in a couple of states where the Governor was friendly with President Booth the army units there refused to do anything to disarm the national guard or to stop them doing things.

Naturally we reported in all that we saw. Where we knew units were supporting President Booth we disconnected them from the main fighting network, giving them spoof data that they would think was real. We also stopped them from communicating with other units that we were unsure of the loyalty of, although they still got all the general communications and some specific point to point communications from reliable commanders. This was the best we could do to disrupt their operations and try and entice them back into our command.

CHAPTER THREE

Problems In Nebraska

About 14 hours after we were up it became clear that there was a problem with Nebraska. The Secret Service detail remained with President Booth as it was still necessary to protect him, even if he was supposed to be temporarily out of the chain of command. Being firm on the constitutional niceties and pragmatic sorts, they were reporting their location and movements to their HQ as their SOPs dictated. This allowed for replacement shifts, medical standby and all the other usually unseen members of the Presidential circus to remain within appropriate supporting distances.

It hadn't taken long for us to get a handle on this, and although we weren't directly reading the messages, it meant that we knew exactly where the security detail were. So, from the White House President Booth had flown to Camp David where he had made his early broadcast from. He'd only stayed there for long enough to use the broadcast facilities before moving on again.

Profoundly distrustful of the military, he'd flown to a civilian airport and had Marine One refueled for a trip to the Louisiana National Guard air base. There he switched to a fixed wing aircraft and flew to Nebraska. He'd been on TV from Nebraska, so that was no secret, and the state national guard had been pledged in allegiance to him by the Governor, his brother in law.

What happened next was more disturbing. In the western part of Nebraska there were still some nuclear missile silos. These were run by the US Space Force, and guarded by some specialist troops. However, they were expecting the National Guard to be their back up if they were attacked, rather than being the attackers. So when President Booth turned up with a company of main battle tanks and a battalion of armored infantry it caused a problem.

We were monitoring all the facilities, so I

was rapidly alerted and watched most of the action on the close circuit television cameras around the perimeter and in key places within the launch facility and its associated command bunker.

I got a personal message from Mary marked eyes only. It contained one word, 'Cheese'. I smiled as I deleted it. It meant that she was going somewhere safe.

The first warning was the deployment off the main interstate of the mile and a half long convoy, which took about 20 minutes to sort itself out and turn into a line abreast assault formation with the tanks in the lead. While this was happening two light armored utility vehicles drew up to the main gate. From the lead vehicle a National Guard Major stepped out and approached the barrier, returning the salute from the specialist guarding the gate.

'Sir, I need to see your identity credentials and can you please tell me who you are here to see?' the guard said.

'I'm here to see the Base Commander, Specialist. Here are my credentials.' The Major un-clipped the identity card from his right breast pocket flap.

'Thank you, sir. Please wait here while I verify these.' The specialist stepped back to the guard hut to wave the Major's identity card in front of the reader. It promptly turned orange, indicating genuine credentials without clearance for this facility.

'Sir, I'm going to have to ask you to wait here a little longer while I contact the Base Commander. You don't appear to have the right sort of clearance for here. Are you sure you are in the right place? The National Guard base is about ten miles further down the road,' the Specialist said.

'I'm sure I'm in the right place, Specialist. I've just come from the National Guard base on the direct orders of the Commander-in-Chief himself. Get your CO out here right now!'

'Will do, sir!' The specialist ran off into the guard room, closing the gate behind him.

'Ma'am, I've got a National Guard Major out here who says that the President told him personally to come and see the Base Commander. His credentials are orange.'

'I'll come out and see him, sit tight, Specialist,' replied the duty officer in the control room.

At the gate the National Guard Major approached the wire, arriving there are the same time as the duty officer. The base officer saluted first, and the National Guard Major returned it with an even crisp motion.

'Good morning Sir, how can I be of assistance?' the base officer asked.

'I've been ordered by the President to take over your facility. Can you please convey me to the Base Commander, Lieutenant?'

'Do you have verified orders that I can check

please sir?'

✪

The Lieutenant was doing her job well. I signalled to the Base Commander to stall for time while they made their missiles unusable.

✪

The National Guard Major looked at the Lieutenant for a moment, and then smiled. 'In fact I do have verified orders. Would you like to see the verification?'

'Yes please sir.' replied the Lieutenant. In the background I could see the dust cloud starting to rise, as could the Lieutenant I assumed. It looked like the National Guard armored battalion had shaken itself out into an extended line assault formation and had started moving towards the base.

'Stay here.' The National Guard Major said as he walked back to the second utility vehicle.

✪

Opening the door to the utility vehicle, the

National Guard Major has a brief conversation with the occupants, but too far away for the microphones to pick up his conversation. He steps back, holding the rear door open and standing stiffly at attention. A moment later President Booth gets out of the utility vehicle. This is an unexpected surprise. But it means that we know exactly where he is. I put another urgent flag on this stream for the Pentagon guys to watch it themselves.

The National Guard Major and President Booth walk back to the gate. As soon as the Lieutenant realizes who is accompanying the Major she too snaps to attention, followed by a salute that her trainers would have been proud of. While this was going on I took the opportunity to talk to the Lieutenant through the battle net radio that all US military wear on operational duties. I told her that the President wasn't in the chain of command, but that he ought to be politely detained for medical treatment as he'd refused it earlier and was in urgent need. However, this was to be done

41

subtly and without mentioning it.

The Base Commander signaled back that he had dispatched technicians to take his missiles off-line, but that it would probably take longer than he had to get them all unavailable for launch. I told him to do his best, and as a fall back to try and get the launch keys away so that command and control could be disrupted.

Back at the gate President Booth started the conversation.

'Hello Lieutenant. You know who I am don't you?' Booth asked with a smile on his face.

'Uh. Yes Sir, Mr President.'

A couple of the typically black-suited Secret Service agents had got out of the utility vehicle and casually walked up behind President Booth, looking ready to whisk him away at the first hint of trouble.

'Good. Do you need to see my credentials?'

A moment of silence, then President Booth carried on.

'Lieutenant, could you please open the gate and let us in?'

'Do it.' I whispered in the Lieutenant's ear through the battle net radio.

'Certainly Sir, sorry to have kept you waiting, I didn't know you were here personally. The Major didn't have the right security clearance.' The Lieutenant replied rapidly. 'If you could just step this way please Mr President, then we can give you the guided tour.' he continued.

As the Lieutenant indicated the pedestrian gate it swung open, the guys in the guard house were obviously on the ball. President Booth, both Secret Service agents and the Major all walked through the gate, filling the space between the inner and outer gates. Once they were all in the outer gate closed itself. As it did so the dust cloud was getting closer, and I could clearly see the shapes of the Main Battle Tanks in the first line.

They were well within effective anti-tank

range, and it would soon be too late to stop them if they chose just to roll over the concertina wire and chain link fencing that formed the outer perimeter. These bases weren't built to withstand armored attack. No-one thought that an enemy could land armored forces in the middle of the United States before we'd fired off the nukes.

The inner gate opened and the four trooped out towards the Lieutenant who was directing them towards the utility vehicle.

'Gentlemen, if you would care to accompany me I'll take you to the main base control room where the Base Commander is waiting for you.'

'That would be fine, let's go' responded President Booth.

The armored force was still closing in on the compound. At about 500m out I tried spoofing the National Guard battle net radios, I wasn't sure if it would work, because their Major hadn't apparently been wearing one, or if he had I hadn't been able to listen in on it. However, when I issued a halt order the battalion stopped advancing.

I'd worked out what their higher formation command call sign was and had subverted it using the over-ride in place on the satellite station. So they thought the boss had told them to come to a halt 400m out from the compound until instructed otherwise. I also changed their rules of engagement to self-defense only, and to retire if under effective fire. I figured that would help even the odds if we did have to fight them.

In the base the utility vehicle arrived at the Base Command and Control Center, which was about half a mile from the main gate. The missile launch facilities were spread out in a wide arc over another couple of miles from the control room. It was only when they all got out of the utility vehicle that I realized that one of the Secret Service agents was carrying the football with him. It was very discreetly done, but there was no doubt what it was, I had seen it before quite a few times.

This could be a potential game changer,

although thinking about it having the football with him wasn't unsurprising. It goes everywhere with the President and the Vice-President. Perhaps it was innocuous, but why had President Booth chosen to visit a nuclear launch facility? While I was thinking I got an incoming call from the Pentagon. General Hawkins, flagged TOP SECRET, PERSONAL which meant none of my staff could listen in. I took it on my private Head Up Display.

'Brigadier Duff, this is General Hawkins. We're in the situation room in the White House. I have the acting President, Sec Def and the Secretary of State with me, as well as the other usual suspects. They can all hear and see you.'

'Roger that General Hawkins. I'm on a private channel and as far as I know no-one else at this end is listening in. How can I be of assistance, sir?'

'I want you to ensure that the space based orbital network is continuously watching that launch facility and is ready to shoot down anything that it might launch. I also need you to prepare a range of strike packages to ensure that launches cannot happen, with minimal damage. It is our own capability we'll be striking at and we need to ensure only the minimum necessary damage to avoid any regrets afterwards.'

'OK, sir, I can do that. Should we also evacuate the launch facility personnel, that would make future launches difficult with minimal damage?'

'Sounds like a good idea, do what you can, but prepare the kinetic packages as well, just in case.'

'Will do, sir. I'll send them down as soon as they're ready.'

'Use this channel, you have about 30 minutes, perhaps less. Out.'

The screen went blank, and I set to my task immediately. I checked with the Weapons Officer what we had on our station and had my Executive Officer (XO) find what the other stations were armed with. I also had the XO work out which

47

orbitals were best suited to strike at the facility and how this would change with the orbital paths over the next week. I delegated a couple of the soldiers to producing target solutions for each of the missile launch facilities, which we had precise locations for thanks to the battle net and our own targeting data for launching from them. Another couple of soldiers were tasked with preparing shoot down profiles for any upward missiles. Lastly I got warrant officer Twoomey to switch off the anti-missile systems covering Nebraska, we wanted to be sure of the strikes going in without interference.

Ten minutes later I was able to transmit that I had a set of firing solutions for each of the launch facilities in the complex, and that the least effect solution was to drop an unarmed missile right into the silo. If the silo doors were closed the impact would make them impossible to open without first doing some engineering work that would take specialist equipment and at least a week. If they were open then it would kinetically destroy the

48

missile, but there would be no risk of detonation because of the fail safes built in. These would probably also prevent any nuclear material being emitted as they were built to withstand both impact and fire.

Moving up from there we had some HE warheads that could penetrate the silo doors if they made a hit and cause more damage than a missile simply crashing into them, and could ensure the same impact even from a near miss, making the acceptable impact error up to 10m. Above that we needed to go nuclear, but the warheads we had on board were scalable and dialled down to 1 kiloton and up as far as a megaton (on a different warhead).

If the worst came we could probably drop a very low yield nuke within 100m of the silo and be sure to prevent launches while not affecting any of the nearby towns. Although that last option would be pretty messy as there would be radioactive fallout from a ground impact (which is what we'd need to do for this job). Normally our missile accuracy could be assessed as plus or minus 5 meters, which meant we could be about 80% certain of putting an unarmed or HE warhead through the silo doors. Changing the warhead on it wouldn't affect the accuracy.

On the other problem we had the same range of missiles, but the problem was that our space to air missiles were optimized for dealing with spacecraft and high altitude aircraft. Ballistic missiles were slightly faster than most spacecraft, and were just within the interception window for the missiles, but it needed us to be ready to plot the intercept as soon as launch happened, and we'd probably need to fire a spread just to have a better than even chance of shooting the missile down. However, one possibility if that missed was to try and intercept with a low yield nuke just as it achieved apogee, when it would present an easier target, and we just had to get approximately close (within a kilometer or so) rather than achieve a direct hit.

The downside of this as an approach is that it

would cause chaos, the electro-magnetic pulse would fry unshielded electronics across a large area, perhaps several hundred miles in a spherical shape. There would also be blast and fragmentation and a risk that the missile we were shooting down might also detonate, causing an even bigger explosion than our interception. Lastly, with the number of orbital facilities around there was almost a certainty of civilian casualties with this option. So it wasn't exactly minimum regrets, unless compared to the likely target.

President Booth spent over an hour taking a tour of the missile launch facility, starting with the control room and then moving on to the most remote of the silos. During this time the base executive officer liaised with me, as the Base Commander was tied up being the tour guide. Most of the launch crews had been told to move away from the base and leave things secure behind them, not forgetting to take their launch keys with them.

The only launch silo still manned was the one that President Booth and his entourage were visiting. All the other base guards had been put into full battle gear and moved into their strike proof bunkers. Outside the main gate the National Guard armored group had been given permission to stand down in place. So they were busy brewing coffee and eating their rations and generally standing easy.

I continued to watch the President tour the bunker, he was looking very interested in it all. He seemed to have recovered from the Base Commander having checked whether or not he was still in the chain of command. Booth had initially taken that as a mortal insult and had frothed at the mouth, which sort of confirmed the stories in the press about his paranoid attacks.

There were seven people in the launch facility command room, a small bunker intended for two people to control the launch of the 10 missiles in the nearby silos. There were security cameras giving a 360 degree view of the place inside so that situations, mainly training ones, could be monitored to test the reactions of the launch crew to the emergency mobilization alerts that made them prepare for launch.

Sitting at their identical consoles were two Space Force personnel, a sergeant and a 2nd Lieutenant, the launch crew for this facility. Behind and between them was the Base Commander, a Space Force Major, Leonard Duke. In front of Major Duke was President Booth and behind him were the two Secret Service agents, both standing against the wall. As I started watching, Major Duke was explaining the drill to President Booth for when an Emergency Mobilization Alert comes in.

'So the red lamp there (pointing) flashes and there is a warning klaxon too. Then the Crew Commander picks up the message off the printer there (pointing again) that tells him what he needs to do. That could be just 'get ready to launch' all the way up to a full target list and an authorization code. Either way the message needs to be validated.'

'So how do you go about validating it then Major?' asked President Booth.

'Well, we have a list of codes in the safe, as well as the ability to verify them on the battle net if it is still operational. We look up the code we've been given in both places, and if they agree then we do what the order says.'

'What would happen if I told you to launch right now?' the President asked.

'Uh, I'm not exactly sure Mr President, but I think we'd need the codes, because we use them to unlock the arming mechanisms. Also we've got a two person authorization sequence, so normally if you needed to do this the Sec Def would get the codes from you and pass them on to us.' replied the Major, looking somewhat nervous.

'Are you trying to tell me that you wouldn't take an order from me directly?' Booth snarled back with a vicious look on his face.

'Not at all sir, just that we have a process to

follow before we can launch. If we don't follow that process properly there are safeguards built in so that either the missile can't launch, or it doesn't get armed.' Major Duke involuntarily took a step back as he answered, keeping his distance as President Booth leaned in.

'Right, so you need Sec Def approval as well as Presidential approval. So what if I told you that he was Sec Def?' President Booth pointed at the Secret Service agent holding the football, who raised an eyebrow as the Major followed the presidential finger to look at him.

'Well, if we had both your authority and the Sec Def's confirmation then we'd put the code in the machine and do exactly what we've been told to Mr President.'

In the background the two launch crew were staring intently at their screens, trying to not to be noticed by anyone else.

Crisis Point

CHAPTER FOUR

Dilemma

President Booth motioned to the Secret Service agent with the football to come over. 'OK, Secretary for Defense, can you confirm to this Major here that what you have is in fact the nuclear football, and that the codes it contains are genuine?' he asked.

Stepping forwards the Secret Service agent holds the nuclear football in front of him, giving the Major (and the cameras) a clear view of it.

'Yes, sir! Mr President! This is indeed the nuclear football that accompanies the President everywhere. The codes it contains are genuine.' He offers the case to President Booth.

Taking the case, President Booth opens it. Inside there is a communications terminal in the bottom portion, and in the top there are three black covered books. In gold letters on the front the books say 'Target Options', 'Authorization Codes' and 'Command Locations'. President Booth picks the 'Authorization Codes' volume up and consults it.

The Major looks very nervous, he's obviously worried about what might happen next, I can see him watching the two Secret Service men and trying to work out whether or not they are going along with it. I have a look myself, the one with the codes is looking bemused, but unconcerned. The other one is playing with the button on his suit jacket, a sure sign of nervousness in a plain-clothes agent, it means he's checking for rapid access to his sidearm.

I can tell from the console readouts that the Sergeant is checking the flight status of the missiles, and that the 2nd Lieutenant is seeking verification codes, ready to check anything that President Booth might offer him. I bounce an urgent at General Hawkins in the Pentagon, it isn't looking hopeful.

While President Booth is checking for the right code I warn off my teams to be ready for launch, as rapidly as possible. I also bring the firing solutions for the silos attached to this launch facility command bunker. I know that there is a one hour time delay on their launch unless it is also authorized by a second launch facility command bunker. We'll have time to stop it before it takes off if President Booth does give them a target and a launch code.

Then I notice that the Sergeant has just put the missiles into a self-check routine, which will buy us another 15 minutes delay. I make a note to put him in for a commendation when this is all over.

'Right gentlemen, here's your launch code.' President Booth tells the Major and the 2nd Lieutenant who has turned to watch. He hands them the book pointing out the code in question, which I can't quite see on camera.

'Received sir, what are your instructions?'

asks the 2nd Lieutenant, taking the book to enter the code into the terminal, while the Major stands dumb struck behind him.

'Bring your missiles up to ready to launch as fast as you can. I shall give you a target momentarily.' replies President Booth, reaching into the football and taking out the 'Target Options' book to have a look at that.

'Authorization Code Verified. Check!' the 2nd Lieutenant says loudly, passing the book to the Sergeant. The Sergeant then fumbles the book as it is passed to him, losing the page, I'm sure it is deliberate. Both the Secret Service agents are looking a little wild-eyed, and the button twirler has moved his left hand round behind his back, I'd bet he's holding his pistol ready.

'Sorry, dropped it, sir. What page was it on?' asks the Sergeant.

'Page 42, second column, third from top, Sergeant.' replies the 2nd Lieutenant coldly. A moment passes as both President Booth and the Sergeant page through the books from the nuclear football. The Sergeant finds his page first, and then turns to his terminal to verify the authorization code.

'Authorization Code Verified, Sir. What next?'

I stop watching them again as another flash message from General Hawkins come in. Tagged TOP SECRET but not personal, I guess he wants my crew to know this time.

'Orbital Command and Control Station, this is the Pentagon.' General Hawkins on screen.

'Go ahead Pentagon, we're ready,' I reply.

'This is a broadcast message. President Booth has issued nuclear authorization codes to a missile launch facility in Nebraska, the code issued is genuine and allows for unrestricted targeting, including targets in the continental United States. The acting President has accordingly issued nuclear release for a strike to stop the launch from Nebraska should non-nuclear options fail. This has been confirmed by the Secretary for Defense and the necessary codes are being transmitted to you now. Brigadier Duff has the authority to order a nuclear launch against the Nebraska facility without further authorization. This authority will expire in two hours.'

'Roger that Pentagon. We're good to try a conventional strike in five minutes.'

'Good luck General Duff, you're going to need it'.

Returning to the footage from the launch control bunker it is apparent that President Booth has selected his targets, my Executive Officer tells me that he'd asked how many missiles he had and when they could be launched.

'Okay, target data entry complete, check firing solutions.' the 2nd Lieutenant tells the Sergeant who is still typing at his keyboard. A minute passes then the Sergeant looks up.

'Target data entry complete. Sending you my firing solutions. Sir?' the Sergeant informs the 2nd Lieutenant.

'Entries match, please confirm.' the 2nd Lieutenant informs the Sergeant, who stands up and walks behind the 2nd Lieutenant to visually check on his screen.

'Match confirmed, sir.'

'Report ready to launch, sir.' The 2nd Lieutenant said, addressing President Booth directly.

'Good, please launch your missiles.' President Booth calmly orders the 2nd Lieutenant.

'No! This has gone far enough, you should stop now.' said the button twirler, bringing his left hand from behind his back, showing his drawn pistol but still pointing at the floor.

'I don't think so, son, you're here to protect me, so put that gun away.' President Booth tells the Secret Service agent, before turning to the 2nd Lieutenant, 'Carry on, Lieutenant.'

'No, don't! You're not going to nuke anyone today President Booth.' The other Secret Service agent has also decided to side with his colleague, the Major looks both worried and relieved. He's decided to draw his pistol also, but isn't quite as prompt as the Secret Service agents.

This last minute drama has made me pause before launching my conventional strike, if these guys do the job for me then I don't need to put this facility out of action. Then I notice that the 2nd Lieutenant, unseen by the other three guys has put his key in the lock and is gesturing to the Sergeant to do the same. The Sergeant was definitely delaying earlier, because he hasn't got his key out and is watching the floor show.

Then everything seems to go into slow motion. President Booth turns to the closest of the agents and takes the gun from his hand, without seeming to use any effort. Against all his training, the agent just lets President Booth take the gun.

The other agent looks on aghast, as President Booth turns towards him, transferring the pistol into his right hand, and shoots the button twirling agent at point blank range.

All the others appear frozen in time, the Major is still struggling with his holster flap, which is tied shut. Booth turns back to the football holder, tells him he's sorry and shoots him too. The major decides to try and look non-threatening and moves his hands away from his holster. That, in the short term at least, saves him from being shot.

'Okay, gentlemen, where were we? That's right, I ordered you to launch the missiles. So why has nothing happened?' President Booth asked. The Sergeant then dug into the front of his uniform blouse to get his key out from the chain around his neck.

'Right with you Mr President, just need to get my key out, sorry for the delay, sir'. The Sergeant gets his key out and inserts it into the slot.

'Key ready, sir'

'On my mark, turn the key. 3 – 2 – 1 LAUNCH.' Both keys turn simultaneously. Then the 2nd Lieutenant presses the red launch button on the console in front of him.

'Launch initiated Mr President, sir,' he reports. Booth is still pointing the pistol at Major Duke.

'How long before the missiles fly?' Booth asks.

'They'll be up as soon as a second launch facility verifies the launch codes sir, or an hour from now, whichever comes first'. Major Duke offers, perhaps hoping that President Booth will find him useful enough not to kill.

Booth seems to consider this for a moment or two, then asks 'Is there any way to cancel the launch initiation?'

'Yes, but not remotely. We'd need to take the launch keys from here over to the missile silo and use one of them in the abort terminal,' Major Duke replied.

'Good, we'll stay here then. Close the doors and seal us in please Lieutenant. Major, slip off that belt and kick it over my way with the pistol still in it.'

✪

I had no hesitation in ordering the strike on the missile silos. We attacked one silo at a time, with a one minute delay between our launches to minimize the risk of the missiles interfering with each other on the way down. We had 55 minutes before the nuclear launch would happen, and it needed about five minutes for our missiles to reach the target points.

I checked the launch facility orders, which I could read but not change, which was a failsafe against one of these orbitals being captured by an enemy force. The targets chosen were interesting, four of the missiles were reserved for the space based orbital command and control system, which meant one of those missiles was aimed at me personally. Another was aimed at the Pentagon. The remaining five were aimed at the five major space ports, Himalayas, CERN, Santa Fe, Guiana and Baikonur.

The first three missiles were all direct hits and went into the silo, destroying the missiles inside and preventing them from launching. That saved the space ports at Himalayas, CERN and Santa Fe, The fourth and fifth missiles impacted just outside the silos, but not close enough to be certain of preventing a launch, Guiana and Baikonur were still at risk.

Missile 6 saved the Pentagon,

Missile 7 narrowly missed the target leaving us in danger.

Missile 8 went into the silo, saving one of the other command orbitals, we'd at least have a place to evacuate to if necessary.

Missile 9 was wide of the target, about 100 meters off, way more than should have been the case.

Missile 10 hit and saved another of the orbital command facilities, at least two would remain.

Before carrying on the strike I signaled the other orbital in danger and suggested that they make ready for evacuation if we weren't successful. After a minute to let the dust settle the second round of missiles was ready to fire at the silos we'd missed. The priorities needed to be the Space Ports, as they were of higher value than two of our orbitals, given that we had both the time and the capability to evacuate these if necessary. Also taking out other people's space ports with nukes was very likely to lead directly to retaliation, and I doubt it would be a limited response.

Missile 11 saved Baikonur, which I'd prioritized over Guiana as the Russians had the capability to retaliate massively to any attack, whereas the Guianians didn't even have a military, they relied on international co-operation to keep them safe.

Missile 12 had a technical failure of some kind and veered out of control early in flight. We needed to spend several minutes checking the systems as this was the second missile to go outside the expected parameters. By the time we were ready to fire the 13th missile there were only twenty three minutes left until the nukes launched.

Missile 13 scored a perfect direct hit straight down the middle of the missile silo. That was all five space ports saved. Two more missiles to hit, eighteen minutes left on the clock.

Missile 14 missed, but kicked up a large dust cloud that obscured our view of the silo. That was the silo that was going to fire at us.

Missile 15 dealt with the other silo a minute after missile 14 had kicked up the dust cloud. I had twelve minutes left, and I needed five of them for the missile to hit the target. We shot a last attempt at a conventional strike at the silo, figuring that the missile wasn't using visuals and the silo hadn't moved. If that didn't work we'd have to go nuclear.

Missile 16 away! We watched the trajectory on screen and held our collective breaths. If this didn't work we'd need to be in the spacecraft within two minutes to be able to get clear. The pilots were already doing their pre-flight checks and some of the non-essential soldiers were already strapped into the acceleration couches. I was waiting until the last minute.

Missile 16 fell on what looked like a perfect trajectory, although the difference of a couple of meters would be impossible to make out until it was far too late. I gave the orders for the nuke as our backup and then ordered everyone else to the ships, leaving the launch of our own nuclear strike directly under my own personal control, with no need for a second key.

I really didn't know what was going to happen next. How could I go back if I'd been responsible for nuking American soil? How could I go back even for seriously considering it? It certainly wasn't something I could ask anyone else to do for me, I had to press the button myself, if it needed to be pressed. I was certainly intending to wait until the last second to do it.

Missile 16 impacted into the center of the dust cloud, and it was impossible to tell whether or not it had been successful in preventing the launch of the missile from the silo.

I brought the Pentagon up on the screen, I figured that they would have been watching our live feed.

'Pentagon, this is Orbital Space Force, General Duff speaking.'

'Pentagon here, go ahead General.'

'I cannot be certain that I've hit the target sufficiently well to prevent the unauthorized nuclear launch from the Nebraska facility. Unless you cancel my authorization I will escalate the strike to use the nuclear option.'

'Roger that General Duff, carry on as proposed. Pentagon out.'

So that was it, my ass was covered. But it took more than just covering my ass to make it fine for me to press the button. I checked with the Nebraska Launch Facility Executive Officer, he confirmed to me that all his personnel, bar three, were at a safe distance from the base, and that he'd persuaded the National Guard commander to take them all back to his base in Omaha. That was all I needed, four people in the Nebraska wilderness, against a few hundred up here and the damage that the electro magnetic pulse would add to that.

I pressed the button.

ACKNOWLEDGEMENTS

I would like to thank several people for help and assistance along the way in getting this story to completion.

The members of Chestnut Lodge Wargames Group who talked through the scenario with me for part of the background (and put themselves in the characters shoes, making it more real for me).

My beta readers, Nick Luft, Nicki Grihault, Jan Caulfield and jrj1701 for their very helpful feedback that has helped to improve this story.

Clare Best, my Open University creative writing tutor who encouraged and supported me as I developed my skill.

My mother, a retired high school English teacher, who used her considerable skill in marking papers to proof read the story.

Any errors, omissions or things you don't like are entirely my fault and not anything to do with the people that have helped me.

ABOUT THE AUTHOR

James Kemp has been writing stories for over 30 years, sometimes he has even written (non-fiction) for a living. He has also studied creative writing with the Open University.

For more of his writing, including news of the the novel (Perfects) that this short story shares a background with, you could have a look at his blog at http://www.themself.org/

If you liked the story, please leave a review, or at least rate it, on <u>Goodreads</u>, Amazon or wherever you got it from. If you thought there was room for improvement, then he'd love to hear from you. Comments on his blog are a good way to pass on messages.

Thank you.

www.ingramcontent.com/pod-product-compliance
Lightning Source LLC
Chambersburg PA
CBHW020313150626
46552CB00022B/2874